SURVIVAL POEMS
TO HELP YOU THROUGH THE DAY
BY MARLENE FABIAN STILES

This is a work of fiction. Similarities to real people, places, or events are entirely coincidental.

SURVIVAL POEMS TO HELP YOU THROUGH THE DAY

First edition. May 28, 2023.

Copyright © 2023 Marlene Fabian Stiles.

ISBN: 979-8223834885

Written by Marlene Fabian Stiles.

COVER ART BY JANICE WALKER

Dedicated to my beloved friend and longtime cancer survivor

Lois Kleiner

The best time of my life?

It's now—it's today!
No point in regretting
What the wind swept away.
Tomorrow's a dream,
A net flung so vast
It's tangled with wishes
That may not come to pass.
What's real is this moment
It's abundantly clear
I should live it with joy,
Not jitter with fear.
Whether fearful or not,
My joints will still ache,
The ceiling may crack,
Leaves beg to be raked.
I can grimace and bear it,
I can shrug it away,
Or fling my arms wide
And embrace this new day.

The Goddess comes Disguised as my life—

The ponytail atop her head is askew,
Her cat's eye glasses are smudged,
Her two piece suit is rumpled and
Her slip is showing.

> She's balancing a sheaf of papers
> And a laptop,

A lunch bucket and a hatbox with a torn lid.
Like Shiva she needs 6 arms
And only has two.
I'm disappointed at first...
Then I gape in awe at her exquisite
Blue-and-gold brocade
High heeled shoes.
My breath becomes prayer as I ask,
"How do you walk in those?
Can you teach me?"
A smile splits her face revealing
Magenta lipstick
On coffee stained teeth.

> "Just put one foot in front of the other, Sweetie.

Take one step at a time."

THIS DAY IS A GIFT

Wrapped up in blue paper,
Tied with gold thread
And garnished in green.
Open the lid—it's filled with promise,
Put thought into motion/actualize dreams.
Breathe in and breathe out,
That takes no effort.
What you do with your words
Ripples through worlds.
Stretch out your hands
And fill them with sunlight.
It's real//its intangible,
Like the luster of pearls.
Taste the rogue wind,
The flavor is subtle—
A fragrance so sweet
That it melts into sound.
Peel back the hurricane,
The roar of commotion,
And listen to silence filtering down.
Step into the light ...
Find a place in the shadows,
The light's dark and dampened,
The shadows are bright.
Embrace this new day—
It's a transient moment
And also eternal, an elegant balance:
The resplendence of day
With the solace of night.

The Pearl beyond price,

The gift so sublime
Is the one we ignore
The blessing of time.
It's measured in seconds
It's lumped into days.
We tick tock the minutes
And wish it away.

But time becomes precious
When it is in doubt,
When it's tight and restricted
We reel from the clout
As we number the days
We have left on this earth—
The death sentence stings,
Vanquishing mirth.

But hidden within
A whisper rings true:
Don't waste precious time
On self-centered rue.
Take the most from this moment,
It glistens and shines
And it won't come again,
Make a blessing of time!

DARK AND LIGHT ANGELS

Two Angels arrived with the first blush of night:
One sooty and ragged, one shining and white.
We embrace the white angel with flowing gold hair;
We'd drive off the dark one, if only we'd dare.
Both angels bring blessings for hope and for peace,
For gifts unexpected and troubles' surcease.
We take the sweet balm that the light angel brings,
Health, joy and happiness—the riches of kings.
We spurn the grime that the dark angel gives
As if it could poison this life that we live.
But buried in grime is the strength to endure,
The patience and hope that all ills have a cure.
The white angel's sweetness
Can soothe a sharp sting,
But it won't heal the heartache
Life's obstacles bring.
Persistence, the power to rise from the dust,
To polish our hopes though they're tainted with rust
Can only be found in the grit and the grime
Of the dark angel's gift through the passage of time.

A friend is a reflection
Of your angelic self,
Someone for whom you throw open wide the doors Of your heart and
invite inside for a cup of tea.
No matter that the cup is chipped, the tea is weak,
That there are dust bunnies under the table.
You can be who you are, embracing this moment,
Discovering the essence of the person
You hope to become mirrored
In the unconditional love of a friend's eyes
In an exchange of heartfelt emotion,
Of give and take as easy as breath,
Refreshing the soul.

ALVIN'S PRAYER

When the sky turns to ash and the day's bitter black,
Lord give me the courage of Alvin the cat.
Give me endurance to find my way home
Though I'm lost and I wander
Deeply hurt and alone.
Give me the faith to know I'll survive
If I make a small effort to just stay alive.
Give me Your strength when all strength is past
To make my way through each deadly morass.
Give me new hope when hope is all gone
Though I stumble and falter and cannot go on.
Through a day damp with raindrops and no Aftermath,
Lord, give me persistence like a gray alley cat's.

FOR LOIS

When I release you, you will return on the wind;
When the earth calls to you, you will break free
As water rising into mist.
Your image is more than a yellowing photograph,
It is etched on the granite of my mind,
Carved by rivulets of time flowing unceasingly,
Molding memory into canyons where eagles soar.
Wind, water, earth—these things endure.
So does your place in my heart.

MARLENE FABIAN STILES

LINKING HANDS ACROSS TIME

The Pioneer: I'm guiding a plough down this long, dusty row,
Got a sun-faded bonnet and my shoes are old, beat-up men's boots
That grip my toes
But I can't give up, got nowhere to go,
Got to work this homestead, making winter wheat grow.
The Immigrant: My high top shoes race up and down stairs,
I lower my eyes when the rich folk glare.
Don't speak the language, but I scrape night and day
Trying to better my life on a chambermaid's pay.
The Patriot: There's no boys in my family so I patrol my block
Wearing out my shoes to keep our city dark
(Can't buy another pair without a ration card)
Then I get up every morning to do my part,
Riveting steel like I'm patching a heart.
The Civil Rights Marcher: Fear is a smell that hangs in the air
Like a body strung up and nobody cares.
So it's boots on the ground, we're protesting here,
Facing down angry Klansmen stares.
The Woman Today: I've come so far, got a long way to go
Still working long hours for pay that's too low.
But I'm running in heels, I'm taking a stand
So I can hold my head high and sing,
"This land is my land."

EMPTY OUT MY LIFE

SO THERE IS SPACE ENOUGH:
Space for the warning morning light,

> Space for the cool of the starlit night,
> Space for the sensitivity of creation,
> Space for the reflection in another's eyes.
> May compassion surfeit
> My resolute emptiness
> Until I am overflowing,
> No longer desolate

In the space of my yearning.

> May I become so much more
> Than what I am;
> An expression of endless spheres of stardust

Sweetened with the allurement
Of absolute being.

FOR BARBARA

Song unsung but singing still
Of cats and cookies

> And I-hate-chocolate-but-is-there-anymore?
> Of toes painted prettily then hid beneath wool socks

And the joy—oh the joy

> Of getting out of the house and into the blue wash of sun
> Sweeping clouds off mountains;
> Joy enough to overwhelm the heart

And this is enough,

> Enough . . . although your operatic voice remained untuned
> (For who took a woman seriously in the
> good-old-boy-days?)
> It is enough that you are singing still
> In the playtime of sun and shadow.
> Listen!
> The silence is colored with sound.

I started through the garden gate,

I saw a spider's web
(Usually spiders fill my soul with dread)
But the little creature wove so fine a tapestry of lace
I couldn't find it in my heart
To tear it from its brace.
Now I wonder how many times
Disaster came my way
Unbeknownst to me,
Who ambled blithely through my day
So arrogantly self-assured
That I would sleep and wake...
How many times was I secured
From earthquake and heartache?
I only know the odds are good:
There are blessings I've received
A hundred times more bountiful
Than the ones that I perceive.
So now I breathe a prayer of thanks
For all I do not know,
The many times disaster struck,
And I narrowly missed the blow.

I WILL TAKE DELIGHT
IN LITTLE THINGS:

A single slice of bread,

    I give thanks for the pillow

On which I lay my head.

    Breathing in//breathing out//
    Standing on two feet//

Eliciting a smile or nod

    From strangers that I meet.

    I'll surrender my humbug self

And fill my heart with light

    Till it becomes a gleaming mirror

That glimmers in the night.

    I'll be a door that opens wide,
    A stiles that overlaps

A stout stone wall with wide,

    Smooth steps
    To let a wayfarer pass.

    Let me perceive that I receive

Much more than I can give,

SURVIVAL POEMS TO HELP YOU THROUGH THE DAY

Let me be overwhelmed with awe

For this, the life I live.

Some days the sun is scalding hot,

Or rain storms sweep away

The shadows I've been chasing

Through a long and harrowing day.

When evening comes and all is still

My scrutinizing sight

Acknowledges small gifts excel
Every daily blight.

I'm cleaning my closet
And throwing away
The ill-fitting garments
I wear every day:
Frustration, self-pity and nervous distress,
It's time to give anger and envy a rest.
Once I am emptied, there'll finally be space
For all the bright colors
My grumbling displaced.
I'll wear silks of joy along with a smile
And gratitude that never goes out of style.
Love fits all sizes,
You're always well-dressed
When you count all the times
You're abundantly blessed.
Blessings are pearls on a fine silver chain,
They're wrapped up in rainbows
Regardless of rain.

> Though there'll always be clouds
> To darken the night,

If you sweep out your heart,
You'll mirror marvelous light.

TWENTY-SIX YEARS YOUNG

Old cat dozing in a patchwork sun.
Pink velvet nose pad twitches,
Whiskers quiver,
Chipped ears fold back.
Old cat hisses,
"Come a little closer, Death.
I can still scratch your eyes out!"

IN LOVING MEMORY

Your precious little heart
Beats in time with mine,
You are the heart within my heart,
Our souls are intertwined.
Our separate hearts beat as one
To the drumbeat of the Earth
The chord resounding unifies
All life in grief or mirth.
I hold you in my heart
And lift you to the light
That permeates our fleeting breath
And dissipates the night.
Time is rushing on,

    Time is standing still,

Though time may melt

    Or turn to stone,

Your presence I can feel
As long as I draw breath
I hear a drumming sound
As heartbeats echo through the Earth
And stars swirl all around.
As long as I draw breath
I reach through veils of time
My heart still beats with yours,
As your heart beats in mine.

TODAY

I am grateful for all the things I don't have:
An empty stomach
Broken shoes
Clothes caked with mud and sweat
Fear that I will not find shelter for the night.

TODAY

I relish all that I am not:
    Friendless
    Destitute
    A refugee
    A pariah.

TODAY

I am thunderstruck by the enormity of statistics that count me out.

TODAY

I am overwhelmed with awe
That I have been singled out for so many not-so-mundane blessings.

When I shall return to the green,

Walking into the fronds at the ocean's edge,
Will I fill my pockets with stones
So I am drawn to drown beneath the verdure?
Or will my heart be light as a feather
So I am lifted up
To blend with wind and sunfire
And ride the dusky waves in exaltation?!

If wishes were horses, then beggars would ride—

We say this old adage and take it in stride.
Yet our hearts still long for a wish to come true,
So these are the blessings I offer for you:
May the sunlight always open your eyes
And breath freshen each day;
May the good earth rise
Softly to kiss the soles of your feet,
May you taste honeyed joy
With each friend that you greet.
May hands flower open should you stumble and fall
To gather you up and help you stand tall.
May starlight glimmer each gentle good night.
May your dreams be a journey of peace,
Love and light.

CALLIGRAPHY

God's laughter is the laughter
Of a carefree child.
God's song is in the rainbow
Spun from cloud to cloud.
God's name is in the life breath
That every being exhales.
God's face is in the crimson sky
Before the sunset pales.
The calligraphy of roses
Is written in God's hand
With the gentle warmth

    Of west winds

Knitting ocean against sand.
In the twilight of the morning,
In the gathering of night,
In these quiet times

    His voice resounds

In whisperings of light.
We say we cannot know Him
Or name His many ways
They are so far beyond us
They seem galaxies away.
Yet when pairs of passing eyes meet
And strangers share a smile,
God's presence overshadows them

And lingers all the while.
We cannot understand Him,
Only intuit with our soul,
As we marvel at His splendor
In the wonder of a rose.
We yearn for Him to guide us
To an everlasting land
Yet this world is filled with Presence
In the small as well as grand.
We ask that night be lifted
So we may gaze upon the light,
But all the while we may be
Blinded by our sight.

OVER THE HILL

With the turning of the season this all too solid flesh
Begins to melt.
Like glaciers burdened with light
And ice dissolves into vapor
Dancing into morning mist.
Desire falls away like autumn leaves,
Is set free as butterflies upon the wind.
Approach the River Styx
But do not bargain with the Ferryman.
Become transparent! Glide across the water. Emerge as light recast in
rainbows
Blending multi-colors into singularity.
Winter is calling: A sweet haze of burnt sienna
Wraps around you like a shawl
Blue as the shadow of the Earth is blue.
Do not be lulled into lethargy!
You have crossed over
And stand now between two worlds.
For the first time, perhaps,
You can see clearly into both.

EDIBLE PRAYER

I know I am molded of stardust and dreams
And that I am oh so much more than I seem.
I'm energy woken uniquely to life—
Although I am spirit, it seems that in spite
Of my rational mind, my sadness and mirth
I'm also deep rooted in the fabric of Earth.
I cannot deny this primordial state
Or my blissful delight as I savor cheesecake!
Now make no mistake—
I give thanks for this life
Once in the morning and again in the night
But nothing quite resonates bliss and delight
As a slice of cheesecake topped with cream
Whipped just right.
Do the angels who peer from their dizzying heights
Simmer with envy at our human plight?
God surely draws near as we partake
Of a generous slice of cherry cheesecake!

PRECIOUS PET

Little soul, sweet and kind
Most precious love I'll ever find.
Little eyes so deep and bright
Fill my heart with joy and light,
My memories don't ease the pain
As shadows flit, I look in vain
To see you prance across the grass,
I'd run to you and hold you fast!
I cannot help but hope and pray
We'll meet again at heaven's gate.
I know our souls are intertwined
Like wild rose and tendril vine.
Little one, you are no less
An angel—my most precious pet
Only lent to me a while
So I could learn to laugh, and smile.

There is a print upon my heart
That time will never fade,
Though waves may wash
The prints from sand
Before a fossil's made.
This tiny print will still remain;
Tears keep it freshly wet.
It is the paw print left behind
By my most precious pet.

When the sun goes dark,
I will be your light
To guide you through the darkest night.
When the wind blows cold, I will keep you warm.
My love's a shelter from the storm.
When you drink the dregs of a bitter cup
I will lift your spirits up.
I am the sound that is not heard
Unless a memory is stirred.
I stand in light so am not seen
Unless I visit in a dream.
I'm far away, yet very near
And still reflected in each tear.
You weep because this tapestry
Of concrete form does seem to be
A weave of rainbow shadows bright,
But colors gleam far past our sight.
These are the shades of sacred breath
That transforms life, transcending death.

Of all God's great gifts
The one most sublime
Is the simplest blessing:
The gift of pure time.

It's a blessing to greet
Each dawning new day,
To savor sweet sunlight
In November or May;
Whispering thanks
Each exhalation of breath,
Standing amazed
At night's star-brilliant depth.
Like a string of rare pearls

On chains silver and fine,
The years are a tapestry
Of God given time:
With moments for joy,

Moments to raise

Our voices and join

The Seraphim's praise.

I ask that God bless you,
And turn His dear face
To shine down upon you
With Heavenly Grace.
I pray that the gift
Of a long, well lived life,

SURVIVAL POEMS TO HELP YOU THROUGH THE DAY

Continue to bless you
With simple delights:
Breath in the morning,

    Sugared with light,

Joy in the evening

    With the gentling night.

IN MEMORIAM

How can you stop up a hole in your heart?

Use a cork or a plug of chewed gum?
How can you mend the raw, jagged edge
When your heart has been ripped out
And torn?
Tape won't adhere, and string will not hold
To tie it together again.
It's broken and trampled
And bleeding and cold.
You wish it were made out of tin.
For a tin heart won't break
And a tin heart won't bleed,
Once soldered it's made watertight.
It's as good as new
With a turn of a screw
And once again silverine bright.
But a human heart bleeds
Because it has loved,
And remembers and cannot forget:
Sun netted in eyes,
A Milky Way smile
And a hand always willing to give.
The memories cut, they jaggedly tear
And they trouble the turbulent night.
Yet memories are the reason we live
For they soothe the harsh edges of life.

THE BEST GIFT EVER

If this were my last day
I would still drink my morning coffee;
I would still feed my pets.
(After all, life would go on,
Even if this were my last day).
If this were my last day,
I would still make my bed—why be untidy now?
But this time I would be grateful that I had a bed,
A pillow and warm blankets.
If this were my last day, I would savor breakfast
Instead of gulping it absentmindedly,
One eye on the clock and the other
On the weather report.
I would wear my favorite clothes
That were always too good to be worn,
Including my expensive jewelry.
Even if this were my last day, I would try to do Everything on my "to
do" list
Just for the satisfaction of doing it
As well as possible
(I would make sure my list included
Random acts of kindness).
If this were my last day I would be keenly aware
Of the procession of small miracles
That make my day:
The warm wash of sunlight,
Birds calling to the morning,
The sight of so much sky
Filling my eyes to brimming,
The exaltation of good, deep breaths

Opening my lungs
And the taste of moisture lingering on a light wind.
I would make an effort to be consciously aware
(Although the effort might feel at times
Like I was balancing a teacup on my head)
At such times I would stop in mid-step,
Astonished by the wonderment of ordinary Moments ... then I'd realize
That even if today wasn't my last day,
This day will never come again.
I would breathe a prayer of thanks
For the gift of life gratuitously given
With so many simple pleasures.

THE GIRL IN THE MIRROR

The lady outside who looks in the mirror
Is wrinkled and weathered with age.
She has to squint and lean and peer
When she looks at a printed page.
Her hair is thin, it's straight as a pin
And turning from brown to gray.
The lady outside reminisces and sighs
As she dreams of yesterday,
When the girl in the mirror had a young, pretty face
And a grin as wide as the moon.
She smiles again, her wrinkles erase
And she blooms like a rose in mid-June.
The lady outside hums the same tune
She sang when the years slid by slow.
Now she wonders and twirls a strand of a curl
"How did I ever grow old?"
The lady outside, the girl deep within,
Look nothing alike although they're certainly kin.
"I know where I'm going
'Cause I know where I've been,
And every new day is a chance to begin
Relishing life all over again."
She's effusively wise, exuberant-old,
Matured like good wine, full natured and bold
Both youth and age are splendidly rolled
Into a woman with a heart of pure gold
Who looks in the mirror—the reflection she sees
Is the girl in her eyes: she is you, and she's me.

THE LESSER ANGEL

OF OUR TURBULENT NATURE

Puts her china-doll hands on her hips,
Tips her gold-plated halo to the back so the Crack doesn't
show
And prays to unharden the hearts of people Who annoy her.

Her twin angel
(The better of our turbulent nature)

Prays to unharden
Her own heart.

LESSER ANGEL

OF OUR TURBULENT NATURE,

Have you ever painted someone's ears crimson
With the Montezuma red smeared across your lips?
Have you ever let the door slam
Biting off someone's nose?
If you fall off your shelf will you shatter
Like your china doll counterparts?
Or are you merely breath hanging
Like a frosty ghost on wintry air,
Malleable and shape-shifting
As you dissipate into mist.
Can you ever become your better self?

BETTER ANGEL,
JUMP OFF MY SHOULDER.

Devil makes a lot more sense.
He doesn't jibber past or future,
Only speaks in present tense.
Devil never will reject me
Like those "Others" always do.
He tempts me, "Wait a little longer
And you'll get what's coming due."
Devil says he's my best buddy
(They are wrong, I'm always right).
He plays at sleight of hand
With shadows
Spinning darkness into light.
Better angel sighs and whispers
"Let your conscience be your guide."
Devil simply shrugs and snickers,
"Forget all that, enjoy the ride.
Grab the world off its silver platter."
Devil hisses like a snake,
"Losers are both weak and wimpy,
Nothing's wrong with a little hate."
Devil perches on one shoulder,
Angel on the other side,
The push and shove between them
Rolls on and on like the ocean's tide.

ARCHANGELS' PRAYER

May Rafael, God's Healing Power,
Wrap you in his wings
And ease away the aches and pains
Life's tribulations bring.
May Uriel, the Light of God,
Guide you through the night,
Sprinkling stardust in your path
To make it clear and bright.
May Gabriel, the Strength of God,
Raise you when you fall
And hover ever by your side
To support your standing tall.
May Michael, Likeness of God,
Be found within the smiles
Of everyone who loves you
And walks with you awhile.
Four archangels surround us;
Bless us in every way.
They shepherd us along life's path
As we travel through our day.
Strength, Kindness, Healing Power
All hold us in the Light
Even when strong storm winds blow
And dark clouds blind our sight.

Blow upon the embers of my dying curiosity,

Rejuvenate me like a dervish flame.
Repair the cracks in the earthen vessel of my imperfect self
So I may shelter life's fire from the torrential rains
That rage upon the cosmic sea.

Help me rise, lifting my lantern

As a guide for myself and others
So together we may find our way
Along this pathway to the stars.

MEDITATION

My bones are of the Earth and will return to the Stone people
Who have fashioned my form.
My blood is living water, ever flowing until it Returns
To the ocean that refuses no river.
My breath is the wind moving upon water,
Forming the Ineffable Name
With every inhalation/exhalation.
My spirit is the immutable fire of the Seraphim—
The essence that cycles and returns.

WORLD, WORLD, DAYBURST WORLD!

You sing to me through my song.
Sun's splendor glistening on leaves of grass,
Waves gathering glitter,
Wind dusting the shadows of hawks in flight.
This myriad world breathes through me,
Gathers motion.
Infinite world, I am infinite in you.
Together we embrace the cerulean expanse of day,
Name the colors that seep softly
From drifting clouds
To form patterns of light that sweep
Across a stillness
More complete than sound.
We hold in this moment the vermillion of a flower,
A sparrow poised at a fountain,
All life exquisitely arranged, minute yet expansive,
This sunburst world shining through our eyes.

KNOW THY CATS

They're precious little killers stalking on their tippy-toes

Deciphering all they need to know with a whiskered, velvet nose.

Listen—micies pitter patter. Look—there's birdies on the wing.

Crouch low and pounce on crickets when those bugs begin to sing.

Doing everything they pleases as they strut their walk-about,

Napping lightly with ears open to every hiss or shout.

Enjoying a sunbath and a roll in dusty leaves

Sharpening claws to razors on the back of chairs, not trees.

Forever busy prowling—wanting in, then wanting out.

Demanding their every whim—they Glare a silent pout.

Such itsy-bitsy tigers on the lookout for fresh prey,

Seeing near as well at night time as they do by light of day.

Shouldn't tell them they are naughty —they were born with fangs for teeth.

But do tell them they're nice kitties when they run to greet

Then rub silky soft against you as they grace you with a purr.

Next they stretch and wash their undies—they're so comfy
in their fur.

Sure, they'll let you scratch their tummies and stroke
between their ears.

Do not squeeze them or aggrieve them, in a second they will
veer

Away and flip their tail at you while turning up their nose,

Imperially assuming a distinctive, sphinxlike pose.

If they like, they'll share their house with you and maybe
share their chair.

Shedding fur so all the world will know—this IS a kitties'
lair.

The world is their savannah, ruling all there is to see,

Living by that feline motto: "I'm the best there is to be."

At Winter's Solstice:
DIMINISHING//RETURNING LIGHT

Moon kisses Sun
Then whisks into darkness.
Sun blossoms with rejuvenated light
Soothing our uplifted faces,
Illuminating our eyes;
Merging us into the oceanic burst
Of gilded energy

  That dispels darkness;

Swells the universe renewed

  And taking root
  In our hearts.

FOR VAL, IN MEMORIAM

Gentle souls ride the soft undercurrents
Of restless time rushing towards eternity.
They are not uprooted in the winds of chaos.
But bend to straighten again like willows
Swaying in the rain.
Their devotion is the mesh
Underpinning both light and dark energy,
The constant that remains
After the storm has passed.
Their memory is a reflection in a rain pool
Mirroring earth to heaven and back again,
Lending pliant structure to fleeting form.
My heart is hollowed out,
The leaves of memory yet to come
Have been torn from my hands
And flung into the turbulent ocean
Billowing toward a distant shore.
The past mingles with what might have been
And slips like raindrops
Through my open hands.

GEMINI

I am graced with dual lives: one in memory, One in present
time.

The first is a life gratuitously given,
The second is a life I give in return.
Both of my selves hold baskets:
One flower-filled, one empty.
Every day my shadow-self places a blossom
In the basket of reeds that my tangible self
Balances precariously with both hands.
Some blossoms are tart-orange
With thorns tucked beneath their petals.
Others are powder-puff blue,
Barely more than a fragrance.
A few crumble into dust;
Most gentle into mauve ashes
Delicate as rice paper.
Someday one basket will empty,
The other will be full.
When I set my burden down,
My shadow-self will step back,
Dissolve into sunlight.
I will step forward—
Eager for whatever happens next.

HOMAGE TO JABBERWOCKY

Collywobbles twitterpate as a foudroyant fumnabulist toes
A wire swayed by favorian breeze as willowaw garboils, blows
Welkin to crepuscular brume, grimalkin-gray this bosky lea,
Too Panglossian to be atribulous, he hums a chansonette, proceeds—
Tumescent boodle's badinage
Burbles bromides and brickbats,
Piffling their dithyramb, a nimiety of bafflegab.
A florilegium of psittacism,
Catawampus rodomontade
To wordmongers comme toi or moi
This lobglolly of persiflage,
Is aubade or mere blatherkite, though fusty farceurs pen a squib
Mistology or witherskins, it all depends on boffin's glib
Amphigory disambiguates all foofaraw and taradiddle,
Consider this a lagniappe and not a panegyric twiddle—
A desdiderum for the mot juste, no tautology or ignis fattus,

A riposte for *archaic words currently sans status.*

PEACH BLOSSOM

Fragilely pink as butterfly wings
Miraculously escaping killing frosts.

    Buffeted by bellowing winds

Enduring Olde Sol's bluster
As a parsimonious sky

    Drips a teardrop of rain...

...Ripening...

    Sweetened in August's furnace,

Breaking open

    As food for songbirds...

The peach spirals earthward

    Like a falling angel,

Is swept under a mulch of leaves
To sprout tenderly next spring:
A symbol of hope's endurance.

I work in my garden

Daybreak to dayend,

Despite the laborious hours I spend

Hoeing and raking and pruning dead leaves

There's always an overabundance of weeds.

Somedays I don't mind though I stoop and I bend,

Somedays it's all I can do not to rend

My hair in frustration—why do I care?

This chore's overwhelming, too oppressive to bear.

My day's futile efforts I gladly would shirk—

Then a daffodil nudges bright gold from the dirt.

A rosebud peeks shyly through calix of green,

Light dances past lilacs in a lavender stream.

The fragrance of mint spices the air

And ribbons of wind twine through my hair.

The garden is labor but also delight;

It's grueling//fulfilling, not unlike daily life.

If I go out on a limb,
The limb might break!
What will I do if I make a mistake?
I'll fall to the earth, crushing my bones
And lie on the ground till I turn into loam.
But is that so bad, if dust I become?
It is the foundation from which all things come.
It's strong and secure, absorbs snow and rain,
Creates a new template that nurtures, sustains,
Gives birth to new life so energy flows
Through the narrowest stem
To a fresh blooming rose!

TO LOVE WHAT DEATH CAN TOUCH

Like an April fool,

    I dance thru puddles
    Without shoes;
    Hatless,
    Coatless,
    Freezing.

I risk death

    Standing under a cloudburst

Cradling a butterfly with broken wings.
Rain falls like shards of glass.
The butterfly quivers, succumbs.
I cup both love and death together—
What else can I do?
The other option is to tighten my fingers into a knot
And run loveless, head bent in the battering rain.
That too, is foolishness.

HALLOWEEN REFLECTIONS

HEL the giantess of Norse legend—

>Fingernails long and clawed,
>Encrusted with loam,
>Tosses her smoking hair
>Tangled with gnarled tree roots.
>She dances life: dances death
>In a swirl of ice and fire.

The underworld shudders, contracts,
Breaks open like putrefying fruit

>Spewing seeds of life
>Through worm tendriled soil.

Helheim is a vast mansion,
Its rooms are dark as wombs.

>There's room enough for every person

Who was ever born
Under the sun blanched sky.

ON SECOND THOUGHT ...

Hell must be a fix-it-upper,
A house torn apart in a hurricane of remodeling
Never to be finished.
Hell is like a novel endlessly polished
Until it's smooth as polished quartz—
The words all rubbed away.
Look past the dishevelment of the house,
Take comfort in the cat asleep on its armchair,
In vanilla flavored coffee,
In sunlight casting a prism on the wall.
Inhaling, exhaling, I grapple breath, then release it.
Happy endings are elusive as moon shadows.
Most stories are open-ended with ragged resolutions
But hope is the fulcrum that holds all in balance.

HEAVEN:

Could be a smorgasbord of taste, sound, fragrance, color—

Sashimi sushi, Ethiopian vegetables, Naan bread, enchiladas
and tiramisu.

72 vestal virgins wearing coin belts belly dance to Freddie
Mercury and Prince.

Bagpipes contend with banjos and harpsichords, Bluegrass
and Mozart.

The air is incense: musk and lavender, aloe and cinnamon—

All the chief spices.

Everyone wears a mask—Chinese lacquer or carved bone,
Mycenaean gold,

Birch bark streaked with ochre...

Each time the music changes we rotate masks—handing off
our old one,

Accepting another. Our hands are gloved.

We wear mummers' robes, rainbow hued and threaded with
gold.

Soon we can no longer remember the color of our own skin

Or individual faces.

SURVIVAL POEMS TO HELP YOU THROUGH THE DAY

Viva la fiesta!

INCEPTION

Autumn comes with a yearning —imperceptible at first—
A coolness that tingles bare skin.
The sudden hush of wind
Invites anticipation.
Colors become hilariously
Vivid and alive—
The dusty green of summer erupts Into gold and russet,
Splendidly golden fruit shatters as it Falls on frosted ground.
Birds eat greedily,
Spiders glut on frantic flies
In a final feeding frenzy before Winter casts its sleeping
spell.
The Bacchanalian glamor draws you Into this drama of life
and death
Until you lose yourself
In the Whirlwind; find yourself
Standing on your head giddily drunk With the blood-red
wine.
Abandoning caution
You find the strength
To make the dark, tortuous journey Toward rebirth.
Vertigo flares as you tumble
Down a rabbit hole.
Hoping you will land
Cat-like on your feet

You trust in the promise of spring.

AUTUMN IS AN INGATHERING—

A catch and release.

It's finally time to stop forcing a round box
Into a square corner.
Time to sort through the contents of the box,
Discard clothes two sizes too small,
Time to scrub your hands with lye soap
So only bare skin remains.
Time to put on a rubber suit and let insults
Slip away like water off a mallard's back.
Time to let grit explode in spontaneous combustion
So only the bedrock of the soul remains.
Time to turn loose of last year's autumn leaves,
Time to fill your hands with starlight.
Time to divide iris rhizomes; plant tulip bulbs,
Time to chop down insidious elm saplings.
Time to take two steps forward, one step back—
Mimicking the gait of medieval pilgrims.
What is autumn anyway
But another station on life's pilgrimage?
We move with measured, inexorable steps
Toward both beginning and end.

Rain nourishes flowers and weeds,

Sun's blessing can blister and burn,
Cooling winds trumpet into tornadoes
Yet Earth massages our feet
Even when we step on a fault line.
Each day we walk a narrow ribbon of road
Delineating demilitarized zones,
Trusting we will not slip from the high wire.
We balance on a knife's edge but occasionally
We stretch our muscles to the breaking point,
Reach out and grasp a choice apricot then revel
In the sweetness of life's luscious fruit.

RELEASE

Release golden leaves, let them fall to the ground,
Surrender to wind blowing cottonwood down.
Yesterday's vanished like shimmering dew,
Tomorrow's a dream that may never come true.
Embrace each moment, although the time
Is both sweet and bitter, like sugar and brine.
These moments pass quickly until all that lasts
Is love that's extended, linking future to past.

REMEMBERING DEBORAH

I tried to hold you
But your name was written in moonlight,
It slipped through my fingers even as I reached out
And the wind took my breath away...

You shattered like fine china
Trampled back to sand.
Emotions pale; only a husk remains—

A name carved on marble.

We soldier on, busy

With the busy-ness of life.

The eternal is too cumbersome

For transient moments

Yet our lives intersect:

We the living, you the dead.

I trace your memory in light,

Dress it in shadows,

Animate it with breath.

REMEMBRANCE

Raw soil slapping the wooden coffin lid
Echoes hollowly,
Reversing the sharp smack on bare skin
Of a midwife startling the first breath
From a frightened child.
Today, at life's closure,
There is no cry of awakening,
Only a sigh of wind
Swelling the sky to infinite blue.
The wind falls silent, embracing earth.
Sun congeals to gold on autumn branches
Holding eternity balanced precariously
In a single moment
Sloughing off both past and future,
Intensifying this eternal present.
Here is where I'll find you
Even after the grave has eaten its fill
I draw you near to me.

REVENANT

Solitaire child batting at dirt clods,
Chasing white cabbage butterflies
That dance on weedy fragrance
Over rolling waves of green...
Revenant child and butterfly
Arise from the dusty field together—
Ghost-white butterfly flutters
Memories from the core
Of my heart.

SPRING IS A CELEBRATION

OF CHAOS

Cotton-candy tufts of snow cling
To pink-peach blossoms
As old pollen decays under the skeletons
Of autumn leaves
New pollen bursts free from baby-fisted buds.
Dawn is simultaneously gray and gilded.
This moisty day is indistinguishable from twilight
Except for the activity of insects;
The sky is big-bellied, fluffy as a muted calico cat.
Temperatures flit like a mourning dove;
Cold cuts deep,
Leaving shank marks on bones.
Rain rinses the soul, keens for a time before time
When dark and light intermingled—
When fire blossomed out of ice.
After The Beginning came order ... delineation...
Yet the allure of chaos calls us back,
Muddling our steps
As we hunger for primordial embrace.

SPRING SNOW

SNOW drapes from branches, reflecting the rising sun.
SNOW dwindles into florets on the tips of trees.
SNOW melts to pools nestled in undulations of the earth.
SNOW crystallizes to icicles suspended in air.
SNOW awaits the warmth of dawn.

To own the heart of a woman is to experience the Divine.

You cannot know the infinitesimal patience
Required for the act of creation
Until you have counted out
268 Rainier cherries exactly
(The number needed to make a cherry pie)
... Until you have participated

    In a conversation with four women
    Laughing Speaking Listening

Altogether...
You cannot appreciate
The chaos of tolerance.

FIVE DIRECTIONS

To the East

Seashell-pink cumulus clouds sail lavender skies
Then run aground in a grove of cherry trees.

To the West

Sun sinks into gold-corral waves washing against
A turquoise reef and a mirage island.

To the North

The wind-drenched sky grays to infra-red//purples To ultra-violet
hinting at a dark energy swirling at The edge of our dreams.

To the South

Double Rainbows startle eyes awake:
One is a complete arc, one is broken,
A reminder of all we cannot see:

At the Center

Ghosts hang onto our coat tails,
Drink light through our eyes,
Relish sound through our ears,
Savor fragrances too subtle for detection.

Great Mystery,

Not for myself, but for all who have gone before,
I embrace creation expanding contracting
With the strength of fairy wrens.
Whirling winds weave the day's tapestry
As eagles fly between heaven and earth
Ferrying our hopes and prayers.
Sunbeams weave the threads of our lives
Into a single web of liquid light,
Spectral and yet—
A splendid and harmonious whole.

Who is this shadow we call Death
That dares to break our wings—

Death empties sight and stifles breath

    Before we fully sing

Our ode of joy, our dirge of tears

    As days like lightning pass.

We rage against the dying light

    And hold each moment fast.

Death plunges us to silence,

    In this we have no say.

Dew-laced grass succumbs to heat

    And withers through the day.

But the Spirit on the Waters

    Still divides the dark from light,

It fills our lungs with sacred breath
To inhale day, exhale the night.
Our final exhalation as life's breath flies away
Merges with the Infinite,
The Spirit that pervades
The stillness on the water,

SURVIVAL POEMS TO HELP YOU THROUGH THE DAY

The starlight in the sky,

Imbuing all the world with life—
Nothing truly dies.

FOR ANNETTE:

Your mother's hands were open wide
With gifts of love and life,
You held your children's hands to guide
Their first steps into light.
You held their hands when they awoke
In the deep and lonely dark,
These same hands clapped in proud support
At ball games in the park.
Your hands were always working hands
That strove to clean and mend,
When you held up the roof of sky
You still had hands to lend.
Your hands were strong but intricate
You shaped three precious lives
With patience and devoted care
And through them you survive.
For love that gives lives on and on,
Is passed from hand to hand.
Love both endures and flourishes
When we hold our children's hands.

A Holocaust Story

Daniel, a face in an old photograph,
Is a memory in silhouette
Glimpsed through smoke rings of a time
Burning with acrid smoke
That twinges the nostrils
Like the smell of human flesh
Riddled with fire.
I can't imagine this,
Or your delight at the taste
Of simple bread and butter
Savored after unmitigated days
Stalked by hunger.
I can't picture your mother's face
Bled white of emotion,
Gesturing to the undertakers;
"No, this is the child who is dead.
The other, next to her, is still alive."
The men grumble and nod, fearing
They will be forced to return tomorrow.
Daniel, you are only an image,
The ashes of a memory
Held by a single survivor who loved you
And holds you in her heart
Even after ninety years.

I SHOULDN'T COMPLAIN BUT...

Dear Lord, I can't handle one more little thing:
Not another flat tire,
Not a bird's broken wing.
I try to be grateful, to smile and to sing
And shake off these shadows that constantly cling
To my shoulders like weights.
But it seems like the fate
Of the Earth is at stake!
Continuous worry is holding me down and
I fear I might drown.
So help me to rise above the roar of the day.
I'm easily befuddled and might lose my way.
I need a respite just to breathe and to say,
I hope this dark cloud will finally give way
To rainbows and robins and skies bright with sun—
Help me to walk, I'm too tired to run.
Help me to hope through the fog and the blight
That someday, quite soon
I'll perceive dark as light.

May we depart with grace

In our proper time and season
When we have grown ripe as fruit
Broken open to shower seed
Upon the attendant ground.
May we give back generously
As we have generously been given;
Breath to gentle and refresh the earth
And smooth the azure sky.
May our life's breath mingle with
The Breath of Life as a river flowing
Into the Great Sea;
Not dissolving to nothingness
But becoming more than what it was:
Living waters threading a current
Through the water womb of promise, fullness,
The completeness of peace.
May we find peace ourselves
In our proper time and season.
Until that day may we cherish beloved memory
Not as loss, but as sustenance
And the source of joy's endurance.

The sages say

The world's sustained
By prayer, by acts of love,
And the faith that opens gates
In heaven high above.
Yet prayer and faith and kindness
As pillars only stand
When they are held firm in place
By empathetic hands.
The hands that pray,
The hands that give,
The hands that work and strive
To make the world a better place
Exemplify a life
Lived capably in word and deed
Reflecting holy grace,
Translated into working hands
That keep a steady pace.
They do not shirk—they take in stride
The work that must be done
From the breaking of the day
Until the setting sun.
And when the day's work is done,
The pillars are in place—
Cemented by a life well lived
And blessed with heaven's grace.

LOOK!

—even when there seems to be nothing to see
Listen when silence falls.
Fragrance evoked by the wind through the leaves
Is elusive, and yet it enthralls.
The trace of blue in a conch shell of pink
Swells the morning sky.
Dew is the nectar that angels drink
As they sing in the dawn's honeyed light.
Hang onto a moonbeam, a strand of sun
Then let it slip through your hands.
Sensation so subtle it scarcely seems real
Flings open the door to unperceived lands.
Beyond perception, in the realm of dreams,
Intangible solids flow
Like the swell of the tide ebbing in,
Streaming out—
Intuition relates what the mind cannot know.

My Mother's Poems: DAY I

The death angel was never at our door
Blocking the light with huge, ragged wings
Rust stained from smoke and blood.
The Divine had already filled the room
With Presence soft and scintillating as a violet veil
Falling then lifting in a moment of twilight.
And in that instant when the gates opened
That divide the light from night.
Like a sleeping beauty you were kissed,
And you slipped away hand in hand
Leaving us to wonder if you were breathing still
Or holding your breath in awestruck silence.

DAY II

New moon rising, waking from its watery sleep
Amid the reeds and lilies.
With the new moon you rise as well
From the hospital bed with its hydraulic cushions.
You could suddenly see the world without cataracts
And move without the grate of osteoporosis Compressing your spine.
You found you could once again
Name the faces in a photograph.
You became ether, fragrant with myrrh
And frankincense.
New moon rising, opening a threshold
With a silverine sliver of light—
And beyond the door of its opening
A vista of starlight beckons,
Otherworldly and bright.

DAY III

It was irrational to be sure,

    My mother believed that lady bugs
    Were harbingers of death.

My grandmother wore a ladybug pin
When a stroke struck her down
Like a killer stabbing in the night.
Now Mom herself has departed,
Slipping away in twilight

    The very day your kind card arrived

Brimming with get well wishes
And Ladybugs, "The little beasts of God,"
Garnishing the design of broad petaled flowers.
I always thought of ladybugs as bad luck charms
But now, seeing Mom slide so gracefully away
Into the peace of this goodnight,

    I think instead they are signs that
    Grace can ease the way
    As we stair step up

From one plane to another.

DAY IV

Your skeletal husk, so winter-withered
Is re-fleshed with recollection.
You become the radiant woman in your photograph
Who carefully chose pearl beads
To mask the thyroid scar across your throat.
You are the mother who kept instructions
On how to care for a child after a tonsillectomy,
Guarding them in a dresser drawer for forty years
Just in case our tonsils ever grew back.
Because—after all—
A mother never outgrows her children.

DAY V

The ninth of July, your anniversary.
You were a bride ruffled in tiers of lace.
Three years later on this day your son was born.
Now this July ninth has ricocheted through time,
Found you waiting with the anticipation of a child
Toying at the curly ribbons of a birthday present.
Death's day came softly on cat's paws
Tiptoeing into a twilight
That presaged, not impending darkness,
But an opalescent dawn.

DAY VI

You imagined that Aunt Vallie
(Dead these ten years)
Stopped by your bedside and nudged between
The nurses and blood pressure cusps
And sponges soaked in honey water.
You alone saw her,
A shadow in a shallow pool of light,
Though perhaps we felt her presence as a breeze
Stirring the curtain on an unopened window.
She vanished when the overhead lights
Flooded your sight with too much reality.
Most days our eyes are too wide open,
Too insensitive to the scent of lilacs
'That could waft us back, if only for a moment,
To a wondrous and faraway spring.

DAY VII

You were embarrassed to wear
The "Aged to Perfection" sweatshirt
Because you thought you weren't perfect.
You've been afraid of water
Ever since the flood of '21
Took away your home on Plum Street.
You distrusted escalators
And were far too fond of sugar.
You thought you weren't perfect but
Your perception of imperfection is perhaps
The best litmus test:
You truly were perfect, after all.

They sleep,

But we remember them
By recollecting how

They smiled and spoke
And held our hand

Then walked with us awhile.

We have not lost them, no, not yet–

They return to us anew,

When we speak their names
And recollect

How our love for them holds true.

SEPTEMBER ELEVEN

When deep despair surrounds us
Like a tower falling down
In steel and glass and grayest ash
And the world turns upside down.
When the anguish of uncertainty
Turns our mortal hearts to dust
And the saltine tears that ceaseless fall
Blur our weary sight with rust.
There are angels who, with outstretched hands
Will catch us as we fall,
Who sweep away the soot and smoke
As heavy as a pall.
They gather up the shards of glass
And sort them, one by one;
Then light the stars that fill the night
With hope bright as the sun.
These angels are not spectral forms—
They have no feathered wings.
They have hands and voices, helping hearts—
They're simple human beings.
While we have one another
To support us through the night,
To ease the bruises, heal the fears,
Understand each other's plights
We also will find strength enough
To build a better land:
To value family, friends and home
As we lend an outstretched hand.
Wherever it is needed, wherever grief is spent

Blessings return a hundredfold
To the one whose hand is lent.

We are one

We are many
We are part of the flow

Of wide rivers running

To the oceans' great hold.

The force that enkindles
Intuitive sight
Connects us to stars
In the vast, cosmic night;

As well as the smallest of lichens That grows
At the roots of a redwood's Gargantuan folds.
We are awed by the great,
But supernal light falls,
In equal good measure
On the infinitely small.

PATTERNS

The patchwork quilt of my life
Stitches velvet to corduroy, linen to gabardine
In a crazy mesh of incongruent textures

And yet

The kaleidoscopic interlace
Of mismatched colors:
Seashell pink, indigo, olive green
(No combination I would wear in public)
Speaks patterns of mutation and a glinting
Hint of promise
                    Of what I might become.

TAPESTRY

We're weaving life's tapestry day after day
Though sometimes the threads
Break apart, start to fray—
Tangling our fingers in knots of soft wool
That start to thin out when we stretch or we pull.
Then strands fall apart till the fabric's threadbare;
Our stitching unravels, the tapestry tears.
We must darn it back with meticulous care,
Fashioning patterns to cover the wear
That marks anxious moments of crisis and doubt,
Patching our needlework so gaps don't stand out—
And still we embroider despite failing light
As the day sinks slow into quiet of night.
When at long last the needlework's done
And life's tapestry is finally spun
It's these rough appliques, sewn both
Bold and bright,
That tell the true tale of a fully lived life.

The angels of the morning
Sing of joy and love,
They bless each breath
That is a prayer
And promise from above.
They steadied you along life's path,
Sheltered beneath their wings.
They shared the laughter and the tears
Life's cycle always brings.
And now as shadows gray the day
They come in lambent light,
To gather you home in encircling arms
Before the fall of night.
The angels woke you with a kiss
And helped you to your feet,
As you walked the final, soundless steps
Your Beloved at last to greet.
Angels unlatched the garden gate
And held it open wide,
As they had in life, so at life's end
They guided you inside.
The gate snapped shut, we cannot see
Behind the latticed wall,
The day seems dreary, veiled in tears
Hung like a somber pall.
But if we listen, we will hear
The morning angels sing.
They fill our hearts with memories
And promises of spring.

HOLIDAY WISHES

IN THE YEAR OF COVID

What if the holiday lights all go out?
Is that what a festival's really about?
We may not have presents wrapped glittering bright
But we're gifted with stars in a vast, velvet night.
No feasting this year raising cups of good cheer
But we can still take a breath of cool, cleansing air.
Though forces conspire to keep us apart
Let's relish the time when we'll make a fresh start.
This season of peace isn't dismal or stark
If we can just hold fast with a satisfied heart.

JANUARY 6 AND BEYOND

Snow-blind and shell-shocked, unable to see
Have you become my enemy?
The terror is real, battle cries swell the air
As saber teeth rattle and tin drums snare.
A white-washed cancer claws/
Gnaws at my throat;
It tightens into a gold plated garrote.
Bloated, embittered
By two hundred years' weight,
We're dragged to the ground
By division and hate.
Can we move forward
From shearing white light
To find stars delineating fresh, silent nights?
The blood of those lynched
Cries out from the Earth
And angels count tears
Shed from bigot's outbursts.
Can hearts be unhardened?
Can anger take flight
Like a murder of crows cawing
Furious fright?
Even if you're a leper, give me grace
To embrace this multicolor coat
That's the vast human race.

WEEPING WOMEN

I will not be crossing the threshold of heaven,
I will stop at the stoop and sit in the dust
With the old criers, Mother Rachel...
La Llorona, Kuan Yin and Banshee—
All are bent crones with broken fingernails
And ragged hair,
Tear furrows are carved deep in their faces
From centuries of weeping.
I will join them and we will weep together—
Weep for the forgiven and the unforgiven,
Weep for the brutalized and those who are brutal,
We will weep until the wood of heaven's gates
Grows soft from the salt of our tears
And the locks break under the weight of their rust.
We will weep until the great gates break open
And every soul that was ever born
Has slipped inside.
We will weep even though we weep
A day short of forever...
We will weep until every mother's child
Has been re-gathered into her arms.

Thank you kind readers!

My writing has evolved over a thirty-year time period during which I owned and managed a family floral business adjacent to a large, historical cemetery. Clientele from diverse cultures who had lost children, soulmates, parents or beloved friends (including the four-legged kind) often shared treasured memories. Bits and pieces of these recollections and the associated life lessons are woven into my writing and form the basis for my poems, short stories and novels. More are available on www.storystyles.com[1].

In addition to my own writing, my long term writing partner Alice Hill and I also write fiction in multi-genres: Women's Literature, Children's Chapter books and Middle Grade. I also team up with my brother Hank, a biologist and naturalist, to write science fiction.

Although my writing is rooted in past experience, I stay current in my role as president of the I Will Projects, a non-profit devoted to food equity and community education (www.TheIWillProjects.com[2]).

I believe our survival, individually and as a species, hinges on the realization that we are all unique threads in the astonishing web of life, connected to both the Earth and the stardust from which we are formed.

---

1. http://www.storystyles.com

2. http://www.theiwillprojects.com

www.ingramcontent.com/pod-product-compliance
Lightning Source LLC
Chambersburg PA
CBHW031434130726
47989CB00003B/1133